Elephantom
Origins:
Birth of an Eco-Hero

MANIVANNAN   NAVASOTHY

DEDICATION

To my Periyappa (Elder Father) Kanapathippillai Raveenthiran
and to my Periyamma (Elder mother) ThuraiRatnavathy.
for your Unconditional parental Love and Spiritual strengths...
Then..and.. Now!

.

CONTENTS

ACKNOWLEDGMENTS

Sincere thanks to Vathani Navasothy at Awakening Publishing for starting me on ePublishing, to April Jonquil for believing in Elephantom before I did, and to Michelle Harmony for giving me the chance to create Elephantom all those years ago.

INTRODUCTION

Adventures of Elephantom are fully illustrated graphics style stories for children and adults, full of fun & adventure, but also teaching them eco-awareness in a gentle way. This book `Elephantom Origins,' takes the readers through themes such as spirituality, death of a family group, healing, learning, duty to ancestors and personal transformation.

I created `Elephantom' way back in 1994, for an eco-newsletter called `Unity' that my friend Harmony was publishing for young eco-campaigners. (I met Harmony while doing lots of fundraising for an Eco-organisation called `Environmental Investigation Agency- EIA).

The original story was just a 4-panel cartoon, but Elephantom has been living in Greeting cards (my own) that I have sent to many family & friends. It was only last year (2011) that Elephantom was fully brought back into public eye, as part of our `Gaian Times eco-magazine'. Many cartoons were created showing Elephantom's adventures. Then I got thinking – he needs a proper origin story. That work started in September 2011 and all art work drawn by September 2012. Panels, layout and lettering were only just completed. What started off as simple story-telling has evolved so much, and I realised so much of my own trials and tribulations, ideals and beliefs have seeped in. For example, over 25 years ago, my family & I came to the United Kingdom as refugees, after escaping the large scale massacre of Tamils back in Sri Lanka).

Coming from a Hindu background, I honour and worship the elephant-headed god Ganesh. And I grew up reading comic books- where heroes fight villains- thanks to my (uncle) `Periyappa' K Raveenthiran, who has nurtured me in my childhood days, with gifts as well as a strong sense of Hindu spirituality. The `Priest' in this story is of course a symbol of him! Sons often take after their fathers, and as his surrogate Son, I take after him, in my spirituality. It is he who encouraged me much on comic book writing in my boyhood days, and this book is rightly dedicated to my Periyappa (Elder-Father) Raveethiran. He continues his community & religious work in Sri Lanka, to a new generation of (young) people even today.

A word on Villains - Well, for the modern era, the biggest villainy that the world faces are ecological & environmental disasters. On a personal level, I am still and very much an Eco-warrior and a Campaigner. Few years ago I founded an Eco-Magazine free online, 'Gaian Times' (www.GaianTimes.com) to share, promote and protect nature, ecology and our fast degrading environment. Not only that, I made a point of 'adopting' an Elephant in India , and a Rhino in Africa, and have a small patch of Land in Scotland- all part of various eco-campaigns to protect them. And yet... there is so much more to be done.. by ALL of us!

So fighting Eco-campaigns, and protecting animals becomes Elephantom's main cause. I say 'main', because there is a whole lot of fun to be had with a character such as him. He's already met Einstein, Mr Spock, God Pan, assembled his 'Tusk Force', put out fires of London Riots, gone for a police post interview and hosted the high level political 'Zebra' meeting – as well as stopping deforestations and Whale-hunting! (You can see them in the website www.Elephantom.co.uk)

So join me in welcoming Elephantom. He's here to stay.. and he will grow.

Mani Navasothy
London
Spring 2013

MYTH OF GANESH
THE ELEPHANT-HEADED GOD

Ganesh, son of Parvathi (Shakthi) and Shiva (in a manner of speaking) was not born with the elephant head! That came later. He was originally born as a human. Born is the wrong word, as he was `made' or created by his mother – the great Goddess Shakthi (which means `power' amongst other things).

The mythology goes that Shakthi was fed up of being intruded by her husband the God Shiva, whenever Shakthi was taking her bath (and he would just walk in). So she set a guard outside. But when the Lord Shiva came through, the guard was hesitant and did not stop him. How could he stop Shiva, who was not only the husband of Parvathi, but also the god of all gods?

Realising that she needs a guard who will not falter, Parvathi set about creating a statue of a boy, using her own skin fragments as clay! She brought this to life (she is Goddess!) and asked him to guard her privacy, and let none through. And so that is what the boy did – when Shiva tried to enter the Chambers.

Initially Shiva's attempts to talk his way through failed, so he escalated his efforts with force. But the boy was powerful enough to stand against that. Eventually Shiva had to call in all the other gods.. Brahma (the Creator God), Vishnu (the Protector God) and more. All joined forces and the conflict became a big battle of magic. The boy defeated all their efforts, and still stood firm. In the end, using diverting tactics, the gods cut the boy's head off! And rejoiced!

When Parvathi heard this, she was intensely angered. Out of her anger came two fierce war goddesses – Durga and Kali, and they began to destroy not only the gods, but the worlds!

3

The other gods pleaded with Parvathi for mercy. And she request that her Son be brought back to life! (and Shiva realised who the boy must have been..!) But as the head was missing, Shiva told the others to go in a direction, and bring back the head of the first animal they see. So the other gods travel, and find a young elephant, and bring its head – which Lord Shiva fixed to the headless boy, and brought him back to life. (It often bothers me that the Gods would go kill an innocent animal, but World of Mythologies are full of all sorts of such violent acts by the gods!)

Shiva then takes the resurrected boy to his wife Parvathi, and she was semi-pleased. Shiva then proclaimed to all the worlds – that the first prayer in any ceremony or ritual should always go towards the boy, named Ganesh,

This is seen in any Hindu ritual to date. People spend the first few minutes or seconds praying to God Ganesh. Sometimes they have images, in other cases, they use `Saani' (the dung of a sacred cow!) or Tumeric powder-paste to make a small cone, and stick a sacred grass in it. This is treated as a divine symbol of Ganesh, and first prayers and respects are given, before proceeding with the main purpose of any pooja or festivities.

There are many auspicious days pooja (prayers), fasting & festivals in the Hindu (religious) calendar. `Vinayahar Sathurthi' is the most auspicious one for Lord Ganesh. Vinayagar is one of the names for the Elephant-headed Hindu God, also known as Ganesh, Vignesh and Pillayar. Sathurthi's are special days that happen every month, but the one on this month is the most sacred of all, and belongs to God Ganesh.

Lord Ganesh is said to be the remover of obstacles. Hindus all over the world give first prayers to him – with the hope and and wish that whatever initiatives they are beginning should go well.

"Om Ganapathy Namaha"

CHAPTER 1
INNOCENT DAYS

Adventures of
Elephantom
the Eco-Hero

Elephantom Origins

Story & Art (c) Manivannan Navasothy 2013

In India... A Small Hindu temple on the edge of the forest..
..built in a peaceful valley, on the banks of a sacred river.

..ideal for prayers & meditation in nature.

art—MaNN

Sometimes the local Elephant herds often visit the temple.

The Priest honour the Elephants...

...as living symbols of God Ganesh.

During special festivals, the Elephants take part in religious parades with villagers.

CHAPTER 2
THE MASSACRE

CHAPTER 3
REFUGE & HEALING

Hindu priests have healing hands..

The power to heal comes from divine Love..

Baby Elephant is better..

Many weeks pass...
Under the watchful eyes of Priests,
baby elephant plays with local children.

CHAPTER 4
DREAMS & VISIONS

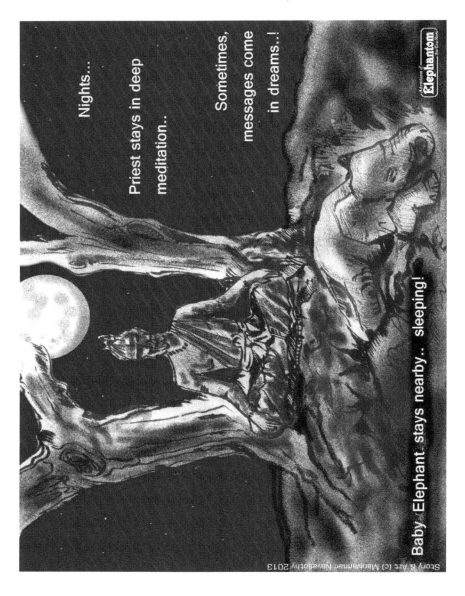

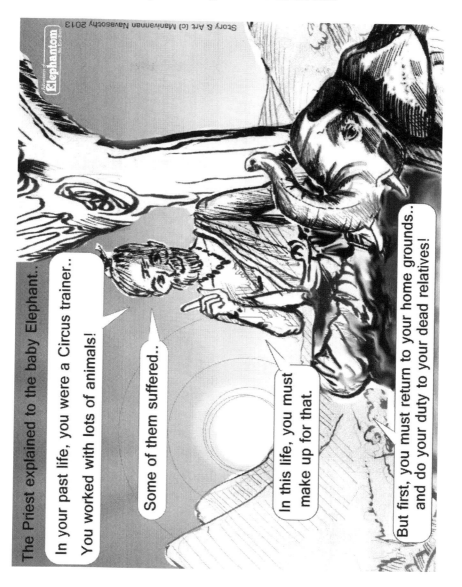

CHAPTER 5
DUTY & REBIRTH

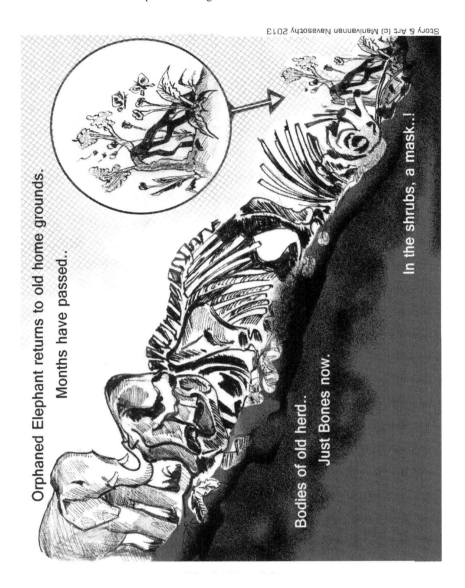

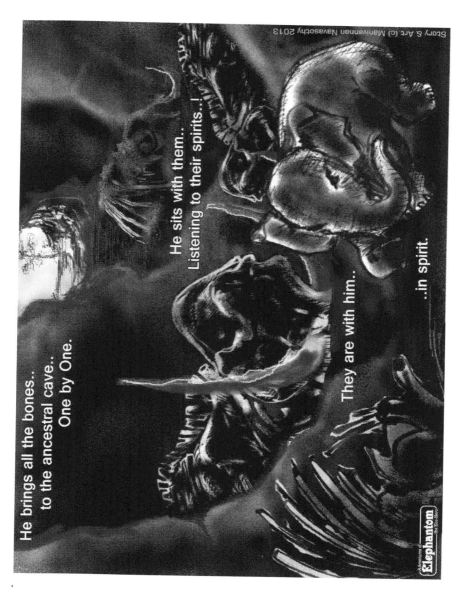

CHAPTER 6
EMERGENCE

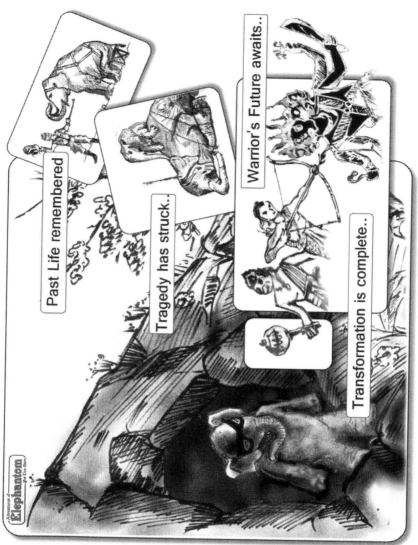

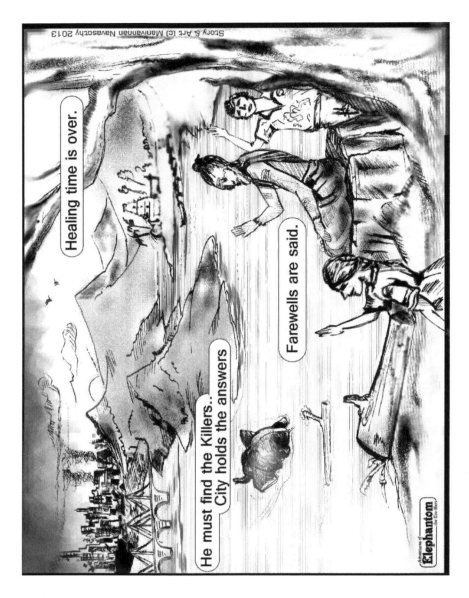

APPENDIX 1
ELEPHANTS IN MY LIFE

Elephants are one of the sacred animals in Hinduism – an eastern pagan religion. Here is a blog post where I shared some of my personal contacts with Elephants in my childhood days.

The Ride on Elephant

My earliest memory of Elephants, like for most people, was at a Zoo, and it was back in Sri Lanka. I do recall one occasion where my parents paid for me to go for a ride on a Zoo Elephant. They are big creatures, and once you mount them, on one of those people-carrier basket things that can hold about 5-6 people at a time, it's incredible – especially when the Elephant starts walking – away from any tall stands. It gently wobbles of course and walks slowly. I don't remember much more, but that is a precious experience to have had. These days people who visit 3rd world countries and nature reserves (Africa?) can quite easily have one of these elephant rides. If you get a chance, do have a go. I mean, how often can one say he or she had a ride on the largest mammal on the planet? !

The Temple Elephant

My second Elephant experience was at a Temple – and it was with a Temple Elephant, back in Sri Lanka. It was a sacred special temple, one that my grandmother & family had to hire a coach and drive a day to get to – as part of a pilgrimage. I remember then getting to the booked accommodation (large room, where all of us slept ..with just sheets on the floor). The part that still stays in my mind is the bathing in the nearby river in the evening. It was expected, and there were no other facilities anyway. And straight afterwards, while still wet, we had to make our way up the mountain paths to the temple – for worship.

It was the temple in Kathirkama, where Priests do not speak. They have their mouths covered by a piece of cloth! There is a similar temple in Wales, UK that I have been to, where they do this.

Well, after the Pooja, I was guided to the area where the temple elephant resided. As was tradition, I was `blessed by the Elephant' (on the nudge of the Keeper, the Elephant places its trunk in a blessing manner on my head!) I was a very young boy and what came next was even more previous now to remember. My relatives told me to circle around the Elephant and pray, and also walk under it. So I did – went in from one side, walked under the Elephant, came out the other side from it's body!

I don't think it ever occurred to me that if the beast had decided to move in haste or upset, or anything of the sort, I would have been splatted in a second! At the time, I was focused on it as a spiritual experience- and still do.

-Mani Navasothy.

APPENDIX 2
ELEPHANTOM ADVENTURES CONTINUE..

In the following pages, you can see a selected few eco-cartoons published on the internet forums under `Adventures of Elephantom – the Eco-hero'.

Save the Whales

Save the forests

Meeting the Witches

Spiritual

Hole in the Ozone

Elephantom

Counseling

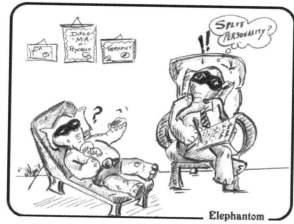

Elephantom

Elephantom: Tusk Force

APPENDIX 3
RESOURCES FOR MAGICIANS & PAGANS

Websites

www.GaianTimes.com

Gaian Times is an eco-spiritual organisation (and an e-Magazine) educating today's people for tomorrow's world (also registered as a not-for-profit Company limited by Guarantee in England & Wales). GT has a set of charitable objectives and aims to become a Charity in due course. Gaian Times e-Magazine is a free online Eco-spiritual magazine, exploring the magic & science of the Earth. Articles on sciences, magic, psychology, ecology & social trends; Photos, Campaigns, Regular Columns on astrology, counseling, esoterica, cartoons, poetry and more. There are many new initiatives, eco-activities, publishing ventures, educational drives in the horizon.

www.EsotericEnterprises.co.uk

Gaian Times Social Initiative for Esoteric & Pagan business creators, online publishers, community builders, Sellers, marketers & Entrepreneurs. Aim is to help & support interested people in growing their own Esoteric Enterprises, or develop existing ventures, fulfill their potentials and their Enterprises.

www.EsotericExpert.com

Mani's professional web presence! Mani is an astrologer, author, visionary artist, esoteric tutor and entrepreneur. Physicist & a Pagan High Priest, he is the Founder of Hern's Tribe Director/founder of Gaian Times eco-spiritual organisation/magazine, Creator of the e-Witch Apprentice

Program, Esoteric Enterprises Initiative, an educator and an online publisher / marketer.

www.ArtofMani.co.uk

Fantasy & Visionary Art, paintings, illustrations, sculptures, web graphics, personal Tarot designs, book covers and more. There are many slide shows of the variety of art works.

www.QuantumPhoenix.net

Mani's personal blog on Science, Magic, Psychology & Society. Started in Winter 2011, it has now begun to have 50-100 views per day! Mani offers insights, advise, guidance, thoughts and frank discussions on all topics.

Books by same author

The following eBooks are already available in Amazon Kindle & author's own web platforms. They will soon be available in print forms.

- Hallowe'en Guide for Pagans, Parents, Teachers & Journalists

- Eclipse Magic Workbook

- Astrology for Eclipse Magicians

- Eclipse Magic Workbook

- Yule Rites

ABOUT THE AUTHOR

Mani Navasothy came to the United Kingdom in 1985 as a refugee at the age of 15, following persecution and racial violence in his native country Sri Lanka. In 1995 he graduated from the University of London with a B.Sc degree in Physics Studies. For a short time, he trained as a Secondary School Science Teacher, before moving on to the Civil Service, and then developing a career as Charity Project Manager & Esoteric Events Organiser.

Brought up as a Hindu, Mani has always been spiritual. Following his father's untimely death in London, Mani began to question spirituality & religions, and started exploring western mythologies & pagan paths.

Mani has followed in his father's footsteps as a Writer, and has written several books – both fiction and non-fiction. In his spare time, Mani enjoys tinkering with websites, gardening, exploring the British countryside, and of course.. creating science-fiction & Visionary art.

Contact Mani Navasothy via website www.EsotericExpert.com

Printed in Great Britain
by Amazon